# ONE AU
# AT THE

### By
### Kelly Hambly

C000243406

# Chapter One

Caitlin threw open the back door of her cottage to falling golden leaves from the surrounding trees. 'Go on, Winston, out you go,' she beckoned for her black cat to step out for his morning stroll, but he took a timid step forward before returning to the warmth. 'And he gets me up at bloody 7 for this,' she grumbled, fastening her dressing gown, and then closing the door behind him. Having moved into the cottage a week ago, she was still living out of boxes and surveying the stack by the kitchen table, she realised that if she didn't get things sorted soon, she'd probably never bother unpacking at all. She reasoned that since she was wide awake, she might as well start the day, so she filled the kettle with water and stood by the kitchen sink, staring out the lattice window that had the perfect view of Grantham Castle nestled on a hill. She'd been meaning to visit, but in trying to set up her new business venture 'Spooky Walks and Kooky Talks' she didn't have the time as well as teach online and write her non-fiction history books. As she opened her Nescafe sachet and poured the contents into her pumpkin mug, she considered about popping into the village to put up posters for her ghost walk she had planned for later on in the week, but as she gazed at the castle, an idea formed at the back of her mind. 'What if there're ghosts in the castle?' She stirred her coffee then sipped it whilst staring at the 14$^{th}$ century building, which was now half cast in the early morning sunlight. She couldn't believe she hadn't thought of it sooner. 'Winston, we're going for a walk soon,' she hollered to the cat and when no miaow or any appearance of the cat surfaced after calling him, she walked into the living room and found him sound asleep curled up on the sofa. 'Brilliant! You get me up early only to fall back to sleep five minutes later.'

Holly Cottage had come into her possession after Heir Hunters, a television show called her up out of the blue and informed her that she was the sole heiress of the cottage after a great aunty on her father's side had passed. As she walked up the narrow staircase with its bold but worn flowery patterned carpet, she reflected on her ancestors and imagined what they were like, their origins and personalities. Being an only child with absolutely no family to speak of since her parents had also passed, she finally found 'home' in Holly Cottage and planned to make it her own soon, with her own style and taste. Although there was nothing wrong with the décor, she favoured a 1940s feel as opposed to the 1970s. The cottage was named after her great aunt, whom she had never met and never even heard of until that morning they called her during a lecture she was giving on the history of the Celts. Of the three bedrooms, she had chosen the back bedroom for its space and views of the hills and pushed open the wooden door drenched in the early morning light whilst knocking a stack of books over because she hadn't yet put up the bookcases.

After putting on her comfy knitted black jumper and skinny jeans, she picked up her phone and bag and headed downstairs. 'Are you coming?' she said to Winston, who raised his sleepy head. 'Oh fine, but you're going for a walk later on, okay?' She opened the door into a chilly day and headed down her garden path to her car parked on the drive, but as she was about to press the fob to unlock it, she decided it was a nice enough day to walk instead. With it being so early, the sun hung low in the sky behind her as she headed down the country road to the village. She'd only been there once since she moved in, and she desperately needed a few groceries and biscuits for Winston. She took her phone from her back pocket and began filming the castle across the fields to show her friend when, out of nowhere, a car horn sounded, causing her to leap back against the fence. The speeding car came to a screeching halt.

'I'm terribly sorry,' came a man's voice from the wound-down window of a Range Rover. 'But you really shouldn't be looking at your phone while walking on these roads. It's mighty dangerous.'

'Excuse me?' she said, wondering who on earth this strange man with the stunning dark eyes and hair was to tell her she shouldn't have been glancing at her phone on what had been a calm road moments before he appeared out of nowhere. 'Before I looked at my phone, there was no car on these roads,' she said, rather offended.

'Well, I don't have time to argue with you. I'd best be off.' He didn't look at her twice and sped down the road contradicting everything he had told her about being careful on the road.

'What a cheeky...' She blew out her anger and carried on walking, thinking she should've gotten his registration number and reported him. 'So much for a quiet walk,' she said bitterly and hit send on the video. *Argue with him? I was doing nothing of the sort*, she thought. As she came to the end of the narrow road, she turned left onto a road with a row of stone cottages lined with trees.

'Morning,' an old man shouted over as he emerged from the newsagents waving a roll of newspaper in his hands.

Morning. It's a nice day, isn't it? Chill and crisp,' she replied, crossing the road to head into the very shop, as it was the only one around here for six miles.

'Oh it would be if I wasn't about to lose my job.'

'I'm sorry to hear that. What do you do for a living if you don't mind me asking?'

'I'm a third-generation gardener at the castle. Unfortunately, there's no money to fix the place up or keep on employees. Well, the few they have left that is.'

'Wow, third generation. I bet you have some stories to tell then.'

The man laughed. 'If I had the patience, I'd write the books.'

'I had no idea the place was in trouble. To be honest, I haven't even gone there yet. I moved into Holly Cottage last week. My name is Caitlin by the way,' she introduced herself.

'Harry. Nice to meet you and welcome to our little village. I knew Holly from school. Did you know the cottage was named after her?'

Caitlin's face lit up as she heard this. 'I do know Holly. I mean,' she waved her hand dismissively. 'I didn't know her personally. I'm her great niece. I can't tell you how brilliant it is to meet someone who knows her.' *At last*, she thought, a connection to her unknown past.

The old man's eyes twinkled at this as if he were recalling fond memories. 'Really? That is amazing. You should pop around for tea with me and my wife later this afternoon. I live just there,' he pointed to the house with a large tree on the front lawn shedding leaves. 'It's called Mayfair. Actually, I'd better hop along, or she'll be wondering where I am. Don't be a stranger.' He turned to go and waved. Caitlin headed into the shop. Pushing open the door, a jingle sounded, and a young woman came out from behind the partition.

'Hello there, can I help you?' she smiled.

'Yes.' She went into her bag and produced a pile of flyers. 'I've organised a ghost tour around the village for this Saturday. I wondered if you could spread the word?'

'Oh wow, a ghost tour? This sounds like something I'd do. Hand them over,' she said, holding out her hand. She looked at the flyer and then at Caitlin. 'Are you new around here?'

'Yep, I live in Holly Cottage. Moved in last week.'

'Oh that's great. My name is Lynn. How are you finding it here?'

'I love it. So quiet, well except for the idiot in the Range Rover just now. Oh I'm Caitlin by the way.'

'Idiot in a Range Rover?' She pondered this for less than half a second. 'Wouldn't it happen to be black with a handsome beast behind the wheel?' she laughed as though she had a run in with him herself and knew exactly what she was talking about.

'Yes, do you know who he is because I ought to have reported him?'

'I do actually. He's the Lord of the Castle. To be honest, he's no Lord, just took it over from his late father.'

Caitlin's mouth fell. 'You're joking?' Now how was she going to ask his permission to add the castle to her ghost tour and talk?

'Are you all right, love?' asked Lynn, looking concerned.

'I think I may have just met him,' she replied, eyeing the fresh loaves on the counter. 'Could I have one of those, please?'

# Chapter Two

Walking up the leaf-strewn path to her front door, she waved at Winston in the window and put the key in the lock. The smell of fresh bread was hard to resist, so she went straight to the kitchen and called Winston for his second breakfast.

'Finally woken up now, have you? Lazy cat. Here...' She put the bowl on the floor and went to slice a chunk of bread, smothered it with butter and jam as thick as the crust and went to sit in the living room with her laptop. 'Okay, Mr. Grantham, if that's your name. Who are you and what is the history there?' She typed 'Grantham Castle' into Google and the official website popped up. 'Oh, interesting...' Clicking on 'events', nothing showed up. 'What? No wonder you're not making money,' she scoffed, shaking her head. 'And now for a history lesson...' At this moment, Winston snuggled beside her and fell asleep. 'Grantham Castle was built in the 14th Century by Lord Grantham as a wedding present to his wife Lucy... Oh that's nice,' she said, thinking about how much she'd love to own a castle. It had been her dream since she was a little girl. Unlike other children, she was far more interested in learning about periods of history than Barbie dolls, but her passion never steered her wrong. After gaining her master's degree in medieval history, she went on to teach and write novels, so she was surrounded by history every day and it never ever felt like work. 'Okay, so it's now owned by Edward Thomas...' She scrolled down the screen and the idiot's face in the Land Rover popped up. 'So you're him then, bloody great.' She then went on to check if anyone had died in there, which she guessed probably had given how old it was. 'Oh, it was the place of the Battle of the Roses. Jesus, that was a bloody battle if there ever was one...' Armed with this information, she decided that in the morning she was going to see if she could have a look around.

It was now late afternoon and remembering the offer of tea; she got into her car and headed to Harry's cottage with a tin of shortbread biscuits she bought in Scotland a few months ago whilst exploring castles for her new book. During the three-minute drive she wondered if his offer were actually serious and was dreading the awkwardness that would ensue if she had her wires crossed but her desperation to know more about Holly kept her driving and who could pass up a cute tin of shortbread biscuits, anyway? She tapped the door when a light came on in the hallway and a petite woman with wavy grey hair greeted her with a smile.

'Oh, hello. My name is Caitlin...'

'Come in, come in. My name is Patricia. My husband said he invited you. How lovely to meet you.' She stepped aside for her to enter when Harry popped his head around the kitchen door at the end of the hallway.

'I didn't think you'd come. Would you like tea or coffee?'

'Oh, I'd love a cuppa tea, thanks,' she replied, remembering all the coffee she'd drunk that morning and taking a mental note to buy some more the next time she did her shop.

'Come into the living room and make yourself at home,' she gestured her to a flower-patterned sofa. 'So how do you like

Holly Cottage and our little village?' she asked, taking a seat on the chair next to a roaring fire.

The living room reminded her of her grandmothers on her brief visit when she was a child. It was the only visit she could recall, and the woman was never spoken of again. She never got the chance to ask her parents the reason why the family was cut off and she sorely regretted it. Now there was nobody to ask and these days she just accepted it for what it was. Taking in the room there was a homely, snugly feel to it that was full of pictures of children and grandchildren that adorned the walls. How wonderful, she thought, to have so many family members but most importantly, to know your history and where you come from. Which was something she didn't have. Only Holly, who she barely knew at all.

'It's beautiful. So quiet and quaint, with a lot of history I've discovered...'

'Oh what part of history are you referring to?' she asked, taking a keen interest.

'The Battle of the Roses that took place in the castle. And of course, the castle itself has so much history going back hundreds and hundreds of years...'

Patricia shook her head at the mention of the castle, and a disappointed look came over her face. 'The castle is in decline. There's no money to keep it going...'

'Yes, your husband said he's losing his job as a gardener. It's so sad because there is so much potential there.'

'That's right, there is. If Edward doesn't do something about it, he's going to be bloody sorry.'

'Edward the owner?'

'That's right,' said Harry, walking into the living room with a tray of tea and a plate of scones and biscuits. 'The bloke hasn't a clue what to do to make money, and he's running up huge bills to keep us employees going, but the money isn't going to last forever...I expect I'll be made redundant by Halloween.'

The mention of Halloween got her thinking. 'You mentioned that you'd be interested in my ghost tour and talk about the area, didn't you, Harry?' she said.

'Oh that sounds wonderful,' said Patricia. 'We're really into things like that and I expect others will too. I've booked two tickets with you for Saturday.'

'Oh that's brilliant to hear, thank you.'

'Yes, we're no old codgers,' Harry laughed.

'I never thought you were,' she smiled. 'I was thinking of adding the castle to the tour. Do you think I will be able to get a meeting with "his Lordship"?' She laughed at this because as she read, he was no lord of the castle, manor or even his annoying Range Rover.

Harry looked at Patricia, who in turn looked at her. 'Well...,' said Harry. 'You could try, but don't get your hopes up.'

'Oh? How come?'

'Well, he's a little, shall we say, awkward?'

Caitlin laughed. 'Yes, I can imagine. So, Harry, you said you knew Holly from school?'

'Yes, that's right. We both did. She was also on the council with Pat here. I'm sure we have pictures somewhere...I'll find them and give them to you.'

'Such a lovely woman,' Patricia chimed in. 'Spent most of her life alone after her husband passed. No kids. She was also a keen writer...'

'Wasn't there a story she used to tell about the castle? What was it?' he asked.

'Oh yes, I can't quite remember now the exact details, but she always used to say she should've inherited the castle...'

'Oh?' Caitlin was now all ears. 'Why would she say that?'

Harry shrugged. 'I've no idea, but I think she was just getting on in age.'

# Chapter Three

'Winston, would you *please* let me clip the harness?' She breathed out her frustration whilst watching the cat run around in circles, trying to catch the end of the lead. 'You're being ridiculous now.' She bent down, picked him up as he struggled and clawed her and fastened the harness in time before he leapt out of her arms. 'Right, now that wasn't difficult, was it?' Armed with her flask of pumpkin spice coffee, she headed out into a chilly, overcast day with the sole purpose of adding the castle to her ghost tour and talk. Whether there were actual ghosts in the castle was anyone's guess, but she always had a knowing when it came to things that go bump in the night. If she couldn't sense a spirit, nobody could; it was one of her many quirks and the reason for starting her own company, along with her love of history.

'Good morning!' the farmer hollered from his tractor that was parked on the side of the road. He was holding a bacon sandwich and sipping from his mug of tea. 'New around here?' he asked.

'Morning. Yes, I moved into Holly Cottage last week,' she said, thinking she needed a sign or a badge, as that's all she seemed to be saying these days. 'Do you own the pumpkin patch?' She thumbed to the field next to her.

'I do yes, thinking of picking some pumpkins?' he asked. 'If so, we're open this afternoon at 1.'

'Brilliant, see you then,' she said and was about to set off when he called her back.

'You're running the ghost walk thingy, aren't you? Any chance of adding my patch to your walk? I was thinking it might help my business. I don't mind advertising it in return and doing anything else I can to help. It's just that business has been slow...'

'Of course I don't mind. This is exactly what I intended and was going to offer local businesses anyway. I'll add it to my list when I get home,' she said.

'Off to the castle, are you?' he asked.

'Yeah, how did...'

'It's the road to the castle gates. Are you going to ask to put it on the tour?'

'Well...'

'Good luck,' he winked. 'You're going to need it. Edward is...'

'Awkward?' she laughed. 'Harry and Patricia told me so last night and to be honest, I've already had one run in with him, so I believe them. See you later,' she said and was about to walk off when he called her back, asking her to attend a village meeting in the pub later that evening. The path veered right onto a steep uneven, potholed filled road that needed repairing desperately, but she guessed nobody had the money to fix anything here, even the hedges needed cutting back. Winston began pulling on the lead, drawn to something in the bushes. 'Oh come on, Win, it's more than likely a mouse or something. Not like you haven't seen them before,' she sighed and tugged gently on his lead to get him walking. As she reached the top of the road, it flattened out onto a small gravelly car park. 'Now where is the King of the castle?' She muttered, walking across the empty parking space to the cut lawn leading to the castle's entrance. The heavy wooden door was open and there was no sign of anyone about which she wasn't surprised at, given the man's attitude to her the previous day. She stepped into the castle doorway, peered around the grand staircase, and noticed a sign welcoming the public. 'Come on, Win,' she urged her inside. The air was cool and musty as she walked across the hall to an arch doorway and when she looked up, the biggest of chandeliers twinkled back at her. Still, there was no sign of anyone in the castle or on the grounds, living or otherwise, but as she entered what appeared to be a library with bookcases as tall as the wall, she heard the tapping of feet on the wooden floor. She turned around quickly, but nobody was there. 'Hello? I'm just paying a visit, that's all...' She looked down at Winston, staring at something between a dark wooden table and a green chaise lounge. 'What do you see, Win?' she asked, and as she looked up, she jumped back in fright. A man was standing in front of her, looking at her as if she'd dropped from space.

'Hi, um...' He ran a hand through his dark hair. 'What are you doing here?' he asked, clearly looking confused at her presence in the middle of his home. But was it his actual home, she wasn't sure yet. He seemed to be the type to live the high life in the poshest district in London, not the grubby suburbs in a cold, centuries old castle.

*Oh great*, she thought. It was Mr Awkward himself and he didn't even recognise her. 'I'm visiting the castle, you know, it's what people tend to do...'

'But we're not open to the public, at least not right now.'

'Eh? There's a sign right by your door welcoming the public,' she said, pointing in the direction of the door which she could clearly see from where she was standing.

'What?' he asked, going to look. 'That shouldn't be there. I told Harry...'

'Harry, your gardener, that's going to be redundant?'

He swiftly turned to face her at this moment, and he had a look in his eyes as if he had seen her somewhere before. 'Yes, he's my gardener. You know Harry?'

'Sort of. I met him for the first time yesterday. Lovely man. Anyway, I'm Caitlin and I doubt you remember me,' she said cheekily.

He closed his eyes for a brief moment, as if trying to extract a memory. 'Er, you do look familiar. We've met before?' he asked, coming toward her.

'Yes, yesterday. You stopped your Range Rover just in the nick of time or you'd have flattened me on the road.'

He gasped as the memory came flooding back, and his face became one of remorse. 'I am so very sorry. I believe I had a go at you too, didn't I?'

She nodded, trying hard not to smile at the crumbling mess before her. 'Yep, you did.'

He slumped down on the arm of the chaise and shook his head. 'I can't tell you how sorry I am. There's no excuse for my behaviour, really. I was in a rush to get back here to speak to someone...Could I offer you tea as an apology...and cake?' he smiled.

Could she be swayed by the offer of cake? she thought and decided that she could and accepted his offer. 'But... didn't you say the castle was closed to the public?'

He smiled. 'Yes, but now you're my guest.'

# Chapter Four

'I'm Edward, by the way.' He held out his hand for her to shake. 'And who is this?' he asked, as if just noticing Winston standing by her side looking displeased. He knelt and rubbed his head, but Winston just glared at him and then looked up at Caitlin as if to say, *really?*

'Oh this is Winston.'

'He's a beast of a cat!' he said. 'I have a dog,' he looked around as if trying to find him. 'But god knows where he is,' he laughed.

'I can imagine getting lost in this estate. It's humongous.'

'That's why we have a trail for hikers with signs around the place. Sorry, come into the living room and I'll call Betty to bring tea and cake.'

'Oh you don't have to go out of your way. Your apology was enough,' she said, not wanting to burden anyone with tea and cake when they were about to lose their jobs.

'I insist,' he gestured her down the hall. 'Betty's my aunt and lives here. She bakes for the bakery in the village and the next town. I believe she's just made a huge batch of carrot cake. Do you like?'

'Oh I'll eat anything,' she said without thinking and then felt embarrassed. He chuckled at this.

'Well that's good, so do I. So,' he said, leading the way into a smaller room off the corridor. At this moment, Winston stopped and growled at something down the dark expanse of the hallway.

'Do you have ghosts?' she asked seriously, as if it was the most normal thing in the world to ask a man she'd just met.

Edward scoffed at this. 'I don't believe so. If we have, I've never seen anything...'

'Just asking,' she smiled and stepped into the living room that had a huge window behind the sofa that let in the sunshine. 'Wow...this is beautiful,' she commented, looking around at the grand marble fireplace and the painted portraits in gilded gold frames. Aside from this the room looked quite modern with a television and a corner leather sofa placed in the middle of the room.

'Please, take a seat,' he said, sitting down at the end of the sofa. He went onto his mobile and sent a text. 'There's no bell here for service, so we have to do it the modern way.'

She couldn't help but smile. Despite her first impression, she was starting to warm up to him. Except he didn't believe in ghosts and now she wondered how she was going to convince him to put the castle on her ghost tour. 'Thanks, I appreciate it. So, may I ask how long you've lived here and why isn't the place open to the public anymore?'

'Oh,' he waved a dismissive hand and looked as if he had the world on his shoulders. 'I inherited this place from my father a few months ago. As you can see in places, it's in decline and needs a lot of money to fix, money, unfortunately I don't have. There are some areas I can't allow people in to because it's a health hazard and I don't want to be hit with lawsuits,' he laughed nervously. 'So when I saw you standing there, I freaked a bit. I'm sorry for that and for yesterday...'

'Oh don't worry about that now, it's done and dusted,' she shrugged.

'I was rude to you. I'm not normally like that, honest. I've just been under a lot of stress, but still, it's no excuse. So, are you on holiday here...or?'

'I live here, actually. Moved into Holly Cottage last week,' she replied, thinking she really needed those badges now.

A flash of recognition swept across his face. 'Yes, I know of it. Would you believe I used to visit my dad's godmother who lived there? Holly, I believe her name was like the cottage.'

Caitlin gasped. 'Holly was my great aunt!'

He was about to say something when a woman singing entered the living room carrying a silver tray with a porcelain teapot and cups. 'Hello there,' she said when she spotted Caitlin. Betty was a petite woman with dark greying hair to her shoulders. She popped the tray onto the coffee table and sat on the arm of the sofa.

'I hope this one hasn't been giving you grief,' she laughed, and Caitlin couldn't help but smile at this because up until yesterday he had been.

'No, I wandered into the castle, not knowing it was off limits to the public. My fault, I'm afraid.'

'Not your fault at all, lovely. I saw he left the sign in the hall on my way here.' She looked at Edward as if it were his fault.

'Is it all off limits then?' she asked, hoping it wasn't.

'Not all. There are more rooms that are in good nick than not, so I don't understand why he doesn't re-open. I heard about a ghost tour taking place in the village and I said that it would be a good opportunity to get money into the castle...'

'I don't believe in that rubbish, Betty...'

Caitlin mockingly coughed, and they both looked at her. 'Well, I run the ghost tour. I'm a historian and I do actually believe you have something here...'

Edward went puce with embarrassment. 'I'm sorry, I didn't mean to offend...'

'No, you didn't. Not everyone believes in this stuff and that's fine.'

'Well,' Betty cut in, 'Caitlin, I for one do and I think it would be splendid. I already have my ticket,' she said, as if it was the best thing to happen in the village ever. 'Care for some cake?' she asked, offering her the plate.

# Chapter Five

'Well, that went better than expected,' she said to Winston as they walked back down the road. 'We now have to convince him that ghosts exist,' she chuckled to herself at this because she knew she was going to have her work cut out. As she approached the pumpkin patch, she waved to the farmer and a couple of teenagers by the makeshift wooden booth at the entrance.

'Want to buy a pumpkin, miss?' The boy asked. He was tall with long dark hair. The younger one was a little shorter with light brown hair and was busy counting the change in the box.

The farmer stepped in. 'Oh don't mind my boy,' he said. 'Some of the pumpkins need another couple of weeks, but the majority are fine. How did it go with Edward?' he asked.

'It went better than I hoped. I'm not sure he's on board with the idea of the ghost walk, but I'm sure I can find a way to convince him. Actually, do you know what?' she said to the young boy. 'I'd love a couple of pumpkins. I was thinking of decorating for autumn anyway. In fact, I'm very late this year. Usually I have all my autumn decorations out by now.' She went into her purse and paid the fee.

'These kids,' he laughed, 'could sell sand to an Arab, except there are no visitors around for them to pester. I would say this has been the worst year financially,' he said.

'Oh they're all right. I wanted some anyway. Yes, we're in difficult times, aren't we? Shall I go in and pick?' she asked and then walked Winston onto the field.

'Help yourself,' he said as she strolled along the pumpkin patch feeling the crispness in the air.

Back at the cottage, she placed the pumpkins on the windowsill and then switched on her laptop, thinking she'd do more research into the castle. She was determined to add it to the tour and was going to ask the villagers at the pub later for advice, as they knew Edward more than she did. While scrolling down the articles on the screen, one stuck out at her.

### Castle Scandal As Owners' Identity Questioned.

'Oh Winston, what's this?' she asked as Winston hopped on her lap, blocking the screen with his butt as he made himself comfortable. *'George Owen, the heir of Grantham castle has been questioned by locals as the rightful heir due to talk that his father had affairs during his marriage to Lady Isabella...'* 'Oh I love a good scandal, eh, Winston... What date is this?' she wondered and looked up the date on the newspaper report. '1939. Wow. I'm going to investigate this more,' she mumbled to herself as she took a pen from the pot on her desk and scribbled it on her notepad. After an hour, she got up and went into her kitchen to make some lunch before heading out to the local pub.

'There she is,' said Harry to Patricia as she headed down the road. 'We heard you got busted at the castle,' he laughed. T5r n

'Did you?' she asked, crossing the road to join them. 'I did, actually. Apparently, he's not allowing the public entry right now.'

'Betty told us earlier that she'd met you. I'm sorry, but it was me who left the sign lying around...'

'Don't worry about it. Are you going to the pub for the meeting? John told me about it this morning.'

'Yes, we love to know the gossip around here,' said Patricia as they walked a few yards to the entrance of the Sceptre and Crown. 'I heard we're going to discuss your walk too. Have you any more ideas for it?'

'I have actually. Come on, I'll buy you both a drink,' she said, entering the pub to a young man who Patricia explained was the pub's landlord's son playing folk music on the guitar on the small stage next to the bar. A man called them over from the back of the room and when she turned, there was a long table full of residents sitting around drinking and chatting.

'There's the clan,' Patricia said, taking Caitlin's arm and guiding her to the table. 'Everyone, this is Caitlin, the tour guide I was telling you about. Some of you have already met.'

'Hey, love,' said Lynn with a wave.

'Hello, yes, I'm Caitlin, the ghost tour guide. Nice to meet you all.'

'Take a seat here,' Lynn said, patting the back of the wooden chair.

At the end of the table were John and his wife and then Betty and a few other residents she hadn't formally met.

'We heard about your little visit to the castle,' Lynn laughed. 'Brilliant.'

'Oh,' she said, looking at Betty, who was in stitches. 'I didn't know...'

'Love, it was the best laugh I had in ages. Edward needed a kick up his butt if you ask me and now you've got him thinking about what to do about the repairs.'

'That's a good thing anyway, but did he mention the ghost tour?'

She shook her head. 'He said he doesn't believe in that 'rubbish', but don't you worry, we'll find a way to convince him.'

'But as for everyone else, I have your permission to add your businesses to the walk? I've done some research into the area and there are quite a few spooky stories, including a scandal I found just earlier...'

'Oh?' they all replied in unison at this and turned their heads towards her.

'Yes, you must've read about George Owen and his extra marital affairs?'

At the mention of this, the entire table went quiet.

# Chapter Six

'I had no idea it was a sore subject in the area,' she said, heading down the road with Harry, Patricia, and Betty.

'Oh don't worry, you weren't to know,' Betty replied, patting her arm. 'Edward won't look into it, I've asked him, but I can honestly say I've always had a gut feeling the article is right in some way, but how it reflects on the family, I've no idea. It's his father that inherited it, I'm just his mother's aunt who was married into the family.'

'Oh I see. Can I ask, have you ever seen a ghost?'

Betty laughed. 'Caitlin, I have seen many things in my time and yes, ghosts are one thing. The castle definitely has something. I'll tell you a quick story,' she said as they arrived at Harry's and Patricia's house. They said goodnight and headed inside. Betty and Caitlin then continued walking in the direction of her cottage and the castle. 'I had gone to bed late one evening and on my way through the hall to the staircase, I thought I heard footsteps behind me. I turn around and there's nobody there. A few seconds later, the bulb in the lamp blows and an ice-cold chill brushes past me. So I'm standing there absolutely terrified when I see a dark figure move quickly into the library. I don't hang around to find out what it is and run upstairs...so yes, there's something there and I always had this weird thought it's trying to tell me something.'

'Wow. Just wow. Do you think I'll be able to do a little investigation of my own?' she asked.

'I'm sure you can. Edward is off to London the day after tomorrow, so you can come up then. Oh this sounds terribly exciting,' she laughed. 'And terribly scary at the same time.'

Caitlin laughed. 'That's great. I appreciate this. Maybe we can get evidence to convince Edward.'

They came to a stop at the bottom of Holly Cottage. 'Ah, Holly. I remember her visits to the castle. She was quite a frequent visitor, if I remember correctly. Always doing research for her books,' she smiled. 'I'd best be going. I'll give you a call when he's gone.'

'Are you sure you're all right to walk up there alone?' she asked, concerned, as it was now pitch black.

'I've done this more times than you've had Sunday lunches,' she hollered back and waved.

'Goodnight,' Caitlin said as she entered the cottage and switched on the lights to find that Winston had knocked all her Ghost Tour plans all over the floor. 'Just...why?' she sighed, looking at Winston sleeping on the arm of the chair without a care in the world.

The following morning, she awoke to the patter of rain on her bedroom window. Snuggled under her fleecy blanket with Winston snoring beside her on the pillow, she opened her phone to see many email bookings for the tour. In fact, she'd sold out for the first day and people were asking when the next would be to get advanced tickets. 'How did they all find out?' she muttered and saw a text message from Harry saying that he and others had posted the details on their social media. There was a side note saying that they weren't all old codgers and were looking forward to having something different to do on a Saturday evening. 'Aw, they're so nice,' she smiled and texted back thanks. With only a couple of weeks to go for Halloween, she thought she needed to go the extra mile, and getting the castle on board was the only way. About to swing her legs off the bed, the doorbell rang. Throwing on her jeans and jumper, she hollered she'd be there in a moment. She pounded down the stairs and unlocked the door, unprepared for the face behind it. 'Edward?' she said, looking at the sopping wet figures standing under the awning with a small Yorkshire Terrier by his side.

'Is this convenient?' he asked.

'Yeah, it's fine, come in out of the rain.'

'It's just a bit of drizzle. Churchill loves it,' he indicated to his dog.

Caitlin burst out laughing. 'Are you serious? Is that his name?'

'I realised when you left that you had Winston and I had Churchill. I couldn't stop laughing for ages. I see you're a fan then?'

'He's one of my favourites. I studied World War Two history for my PhD.' She knelt. 'Hello Churchill, would you like some water or have you had enough being out in that downpour...'

'Drizzle,' Edward said with a smile.

'Oh okay, drizzle then. Would you like a coffee?' she yawned. 'Sorry, I haven't long woken. I've been trying to get things sorted for Saturday, you know, learning my lines and all that.'

'I'd love a coffee, thanks. How's it going anyway? Have you sold many tickets?'

'Sold out as of this morning,' she beamed, stepping into the kitchen. 'Oh take a seat. Did you come by for anything in particular?' she asked, hoping he may have changed his mind about the tour.

'That's brilliant news. Yes, I wondered if you and Winston wanted to come for a stroll around the castle grounds. I feel I still owe you for my appalling behaviour.'

Realising she only had granules and nothing else, she poured it into a mug and hoped he wouldn't notice. 'I said it's fine, no harm done.' She handed him the mug and sat down on the chair.

'This place hasn't changed. Still got her flowered wallpaper,' he commented, looking up at the fireplace.

'Well I only moved in last week and I've not had time for decorating.'

'Gosh, I'm sorry, I'm being rude again. I think I should shut up and not say another word,' he laughed nervously.

Caitlin smiled. 'No, it's fine. I really haven't had a moment to do anything as you can see,' she gestured to the boxes on the floor. 'So, do you want to take that walk now?' she asked, grabbing Winston's lead from the fireplace.

'Yes, if you'd like to join me,' he stood up. 'Thanks for the coffee. I much prefer the sachets,' he said and to her surprise, he took both their mugs out into the kitchen. 'Sorry, being here reminds me of when I was a kid. Holly was like a grandmother to me, and she let me treat this house as my own. Old habits and that.'

'What was she like?' she asked, slipping her foot into her wellingtons as she figured in this weather, the ground would be like a bog.

'She reminds me of you, actually.'

'Oh?' She looked up in surprise and wobbled on one leg. Edward swiftly reached out, grabbed her arm, and steadied her.

'Thanks.' She pushed her foot into the boot and called Winston.

'She was a very intelligent woman, like you. Loved books and writing but what she wrote I have no idea because she didn't publish anything. I wonder where her work is...' he looked around the living room.

'There're a few boxes in the attic, I'll take a look one day,' she said, getting Winston into his harness.

'Let me help,' he said and held Winston, who immediately became still and looked at Caitlin as if to say: *who does he think he is*?

'Well you're honoured because he doesn't really let anyone else touch him.'

Edward laughed. 'Maybe it's because he's afraid of me.'

*That wouldn't surprise me*, she thought, but even she had to admit, her opinion had changed somewhat since their first meeting in the car.

# Chapter Seven

'So, Edward, what is it that you do apart from owning the grandest building in the village?' she asked, and he chuckled at this as Churchill kept going up to Winston, who mewed and walked away in the opposite direction.

'Would you believe I'm a lawyer?' He said this as if embarrassed by his profession.

'Oh really?' she said, surprised, as she honestly didn't think he had a profession at all and lived off his family's money. How wrong was she again?

'My father's idea, not mine, although I don't really begrudge him for it. I would've preferred to have studied my first love, architecture. Perhaps if I had the skill, I could've fixed this place up,' he pointed towards the castle looming at the top end of the road. She didn't know whether broaching the subject of the ghost tour and the plans she had was a good idea at this point, as he clearly had an issue with it. What the issue was, she didn't know, but planned to find out. 'Here's the trail,' he pointed to a wooden sign on a worn patch of grass. 'This will take us around the grounds and arrive at the kitchen door for a hot cuppa and a sandwich,' he laughed. 'That's if you want to join me for tea, that is.'

'Sounds fabulous, can't wait. Can we, Win?' she said with a smile as the cat looked back at her with a scowl.

'Your cat looks annoyed all the time.'

'He's a creature of comfort, unfortunately. I have to make him take walks because he was slightly overweight on his last visit to the vets.'

Edward burst out laughing at this. 'Sorry, I didn't mean to laugh, it's just that he's very comical.'

'Oh yes, he's a stand-up comedian all right, especially at 3 in the morning. Oh but I love him anyway. He's all I got...'

'Really?' he asked.

'Yep.'

Copes of trees were coming up ahead, surrounding a lake. Edward veered towards them. 'No family?'

'Nobody. Just me and Winston now.'

'Sorry to hear that. I've only got Betty too.'

'Nah, it's fine. I'm used to it now. After my father died, it was weird at first to have nobody to turn to, but you somehow find peace with loneliness. Not that I'm lonely.' She looked down at Winston.

Edward came to a sudden stop. 'I've just remembered. I have pictures of Holly somewhere in the castle. Let me ask Betty if she can find them before we get back.' He went on his phone and sent a text.

'It would be lovely to see her face. Do you have a wife? Kids?' she asked as they carried on walking across the boggy grass.

'No. I've been far too busy living the corporate life, I'm afraid, trying to impress my father but then he passed away last year, and this place came into my hands, and I've been trying to decide what to do with it since. Talk about a bloody burden. I had no idea it was in such disrepair until I had the surveyors out.'

She thought now was the time to ask about the tour when she heard Harry shouting 'hello' as he was approaching them from the woodland area in his green overalls and carrying a chainsaw.

'Morning, Harry. You look like you've been busy,' she said with a nod to the saw in his hands.

'Morning, Caitlin, Edward...' he said, looking a bit taken aback to see them together. 'I've had to take a few of the old trees down, Ed, because they looked like they may impose a danger on the public.'

'But you don't let the public in here,' she said, and Harry looked at Edward as if to say that's true.

'We do get trespassers in here. I've seen them. But at least that's sorted, thanks Harry.'

'No worries. I'm off to get Betty's famous bacon butties and a mug of tea. I'll see you both later.'

As Harry headed towards the castle, Caitlin said, 'It's a shame about having to close this place off. Have you thought more about my idea of bringing more people in here, perhaps offer them a packaged deal? A night in the castle, breakfast, and a ghost tour, but we can call it a history...'

'Sorry,' he butted in. 'I don't believe in ghosts, and I don't think they would want to stay in a place like this if they were real.'

She wondered why he was so against it when he clearly wanted to save the castle from yet more ruin.

'I just thought it would bring in good money,' she said, but he gave her a look to say that the conversation was done.

# Chapter Eight

'And here we have the kitchen,' Edward pushed open the red door to the smell of brewing coffee and cake baking in the oven. It had a cottage country feel, with wooden cupboards and an AGA cooker. Betty was standing behind the island dusting icing on a cake. She looked up as they entered.

'There you are. How was the walk?' she asked, wiping her hands on a tea towel.

'Boggy,' Caitlin replied and picked up Winston, who Betty immediately made a fuss over and fed him a slice of ham. 'I think he has a new best friend,' she laughed.

'Oh I do love cats,' she said and as she did, Churchill came up to her and put his paws on her legs. 'And you too.'

Edward removed his boots by the door and asked if she had managed to find any pictures of Holly.

'Yes, I did. I left them in the living room for you. Would you like me to fetch the coffee and cake through too?' She asked.

'I can do that, it's not a problem,' she offered. There was just something about people waiting on you that made her feel uncomfortable even in a castle, but even more so in a castle that was falling apart, and the employees were about to lose their jobs. 'Can I take a piece of this?' she asked, picking up the fruit cake.

'Course you can. Help yourself. Oh, Edward there was a call for you in your office from a Mr Ashton. He said it's urgent.'

At the mention of his name, Caitlin saw Edward stiffen. 'Thanks, Betty, but I'll call him back later on. I've a guest right now and it'll be rude of me...'

'It's fine,' Caitlin said with a mouthful of cake. 'I can hang about here if you want to make the call.'

Edward laughed. 'If I leave you here, I doubt there'll be any cake left,' he winked to show he was joking. 'Come on, let's take it to the living room...' He put everything on a tray and led the way. Caitlin looked at Betty, who was smiling.

'I've never seen him like this before,' she whispered.

'Like what? Helpful?'

'I noticed a change in him when he met you. Oh come on, haven't you noticed? Asking you for a walk this morning?'

She didn't know what to say. The last thing she imagined was that he liked her in that way after their first introduction. Maybe she had been too preoccupied with the tour to notice anyway if he had. The question she needed to ask herself was did she like him more than a friend? 'Wow, Betty I don't know...'

'Just go get your coffee before it gets cold and shush about this evening, all right? Once we get our proof, he can't stop us and may not think about selling the place. What I think he needs is encouragement and support. I think he's not been himself since he got this place.'

'I can imagine. It'll be a burden on anyone,' she replied, looking up at the cracked ceiling.

'Ah there you are. I thought you decided to go home instead,' he laughed, but she could tell he wasn't really joking. The fire was roaring, taking the damp chill off the air and the lamp was on beside the sofa as it had become overcast, plunging the already dark castle into a darker abyss.

'Looks cosy, very autumnal,' she commented, thinking it could use a few more plump cushions and nice fabrics to take the edge off. She sat opposite him and began cutting the cake into wedges. 'So you said you had pictures of Holly?'

'Oh yes, here they are.' He picked up a handful of photos from the sofa and passed them to her. 'Lovely woman. Unfortunately, I couldn't make it back for the funeral...'

'Oh my god, she looks like my dad a bit,' she gasped.

Edward poured the coffee. 'She loved the castle and would often sit in the library writing or researching. Remind me to show you the library properly,' he said, as if he assumed she'd be wanting to come back and enjoy his company.

'Would you mind if I borrowed these to have copied?' she asked, thinking she'd frame them along with her parents' pictures.

'Not at all. So tell me more about Caitlin then,' he asked, sitting back against the sofa. 'Besides the ghosts,' he smiled.

'Not much to say, really. I just write, read, and teach. Pretty boring. Oh and walk Winston when I can get the leash on him.'

'I wouldn't say you're boring,' he said, then swiftly took a sip of his coffee with a lingering look at her from over the rim of the mug.

'Oh, unfortunately there are a lot of people who think history is boring, believe me.'

'No, I mean you, as a person. I think you're the most interesting person in the village,' he said, but there was a touch of sadness in his eyes as he said this, and she didn't understand the meaning of it.

# Chapter Nine

'I feel a bit guilty now going behind his back,' she said to Lynn, who was stacking a fresh batch of bread on the counter.

Lynn laughed, broke off some bread and opened a jar of jam. 'Don't be. He won't be there and it's a bit of fun. I'd love to come along...'

'Why don't you? It'll be fun.'

'Could I? Yes, why not then. It'll be a laugh. Try this...' she said, handing her a chunk of bread with orange-coloured jam laying thick on the top. 'It's pumpkin jam I made from the farm. What do you honestly think?' she said, then bit her lip nervously as she took a bite.

'Oh wow,' she said as the warm bread and the tangy jam exploded in her mouth. 'This is divine. What's that spice I can taste?'

'A pinch of ginger. Do you think it's all right for selling in the shop?'

'Absolutely. Give me two jars before it sells out. Oh and another loaf, please.'

'I thought it may help John out,' she said, putting two jars in Caitlin's bag. 'All the proceeds go to him and the kids. We've all had a rough time of it, to be honest, since the castle has been closed. It was our bread and butter for years, it's what people came for, you know.'

Getting her card out of her purse, she agreed. 'We really must try and convince him that within means he can still have tours. I honestly don't know what his problem is, but I do know he's considering selling...'

Lynn gasped. 'No!'

'Well, please don't quote me because all I heard was the mention of a lawyer. I guess tonight is the night to prove it,' she said, grabbing her bad from the counter. 'Shall I meet you at mine, say about 7?'

'Seven it is. I'll download the Spirit App,' she chuckled. 'I ain't afraid of no ghost,' she intoned and did an impression of a Ghostbuster holding a proton gun.

'My favourite film too,' she laughed as she headed out of the shop. Strolling along the quiet road home, she wondered about Holly and her love of the castle, not to mention her writings and research that she kept secret. What was she writing and researching about? She had to find out, and knowing the attic was the only place that wasn't cleared, she decided she needed to pay it a visit.

The evening was drawing in and it was only 4.30, so she switched on her little electric fire and salt lamp, which gave the small living area a warm, cosy glow and went to make a hot chocolate before heading upstairs to the attic. Winston was already sitting on the countertop, silently demanding his supper, and mewed when she didn't hurry to squeeze the contents of the packet into his bowl quick enough. 'All right, all right, your royal highness. Maybe it's you that should be living in the castle, not Edward,' she laughed at this, then remembered the article she'd found about the ownership. *What was that about?*' she wondered, carrying her mug of chocolate up the stairs. *And why is it such a sore subject to talk about amongst the residents?* She put her mug on the top stair and pulled down the attic door, which doubled as a ladder and armed with the torch on her mobile, she made her way up into the darkness. A chill brushed her face, and she panned the torch around to find just two small boxes and nothing else. 'Wow. This must be the cleanest attic in the world,' she laughed to herself and heaved herself up. She pulled the box closer and noticed it was securely taped, so she checked the other and that was too. After hauling them down the ladder, she took them into her room and switched on the light and at this point Winston pounced on the bed, giving them a good sniff.

'What do you think we'll find?' she asked him whilst taking a pair of scissors from her vanity case and ripping it open. Winston stood guard staring at her, lifting the lid to find piles of notebooks of varying colour, thickness, and hardness. 'When he said she was a writer, he meant it, eh Win?' she said, thinking she must love writing stories, but when she turned the page of a hardback book with the date 2004, she gasped.

# Chapter Ten

' *My research into the legal owners of the castle has led me to the solid proof that I am the rightful heir as I have been told by my dear mother since I could talk. My father was shunned from the family over a dispute, and it was passed to the other son...*'

'Oh my god, Winston. Can you believe this?' She showed him the page and realised cats can't read and then paced the room squeezing the bridge of her nose. 'If this is true, which I suspect it is, then that means...and that means also that Edward and I related! And I own the castle. Maybe. Possibly...' She sat down on the sofa in shock. For the next ten minutes she sat trying to absorb the information while Winston looked on from the arm of the chair. 'Okay,' she said, coming around to the idea that she could potentially inherit a castle. 'I need to figure out what to do about this. I can't just charge in there like a knight in armour and demand they hand me the keys. You know what, Win? I think I better have a quiet chat with Betty. Maybe Holly wasn't really all there.'

Just then, a text message comes through.

**Hi Caitlin, Ed has gone on his trip, so the castle is free. Betty.**

Realising the time, she got her coat from the back of the chair where she left it, put it on, and walked out of the cottage in a daze.

'Are you ready to bust some ghosts?' Lynn said, giving her a fright on the doorstep.

'Oh my god, Lynn, you scared me half to death,' she laughed, placing a hand on her pounding heart.

'You sure were miles away, love. Is everything okay?' said Lynn, wearing her big woolly coat and carrying a bag that looked like it contained more than two bottles of wine.

She didn't really want to confide in Lynn just yet, so brushed off her concern. 'Yes, just had a long day, that's all. Come on, Betty said he's left.'

'Always swanning off to London these days I notice. Not that it's any of my business of course, just being a shopkeeper you hear and know everything,' she said as they walked down the path with the torches on their mobiles. 'Gosh, it's so dark...'

'I need to invest in solar lights, don't I?' Caitlin said, realising for the first time how dark it actually gets in the countryside. As for Edward, she already knew why he was going to London. If he wasn't selling the property, is it possible that he was trying to find the answers to the scandal? Did he already know and was trying to protect his inheritance?

'Edward's gorgeous, isn't he? I'm surprised nobody's snatched him up yet.'

Walking up the road towards the castle with only two beams of light breaking the darkness, Caitlin felt stuck for words, knowing they could be cousins...or something. 'If you like that sort of thing,' she answered, and quickly changed the subject. 'Did you know Edward's father then?' she enquired, trying to find out how they could be related.

'Nobody knew him, if I'm honest. Kept himself to himself but saying that he did do quite a bit of charity work and gave a lot to the village.'

'Oh right,' she said surprised to hear it considering. She expected to hear that he was a monster that stole people's heritages, but then perhaps he knew and felt guilty? As she had to remind herself, there were always two sides to a story, one not always true but a story nonetheless, she had to find out to put the puzzle together. 'He must've come from a wealthy family then?' she asked, digging for more information as they came to the castle door.

'Yes, he did, but there has been talks that he shouldn't have inherited it and that's where the scandal came in that people don't like to talk about.'

'Yes, about that, why is that?'

'The thing is, he helped so many out in times of trouble, financially and otherwise, that they don't like to bad mouth him. In fact, if it is true, and he wasn't supposed to inherit his fortune, then is he really to blame? That should lie with his father then, shouldn't it?'

She had to admit that Lynn was right except the scandal involved extra marital affairs that may or may not have resulted in children... 'Oh this is making sense a bit,' she said when the door swung open with a creak and Betty's face appeared from behind it.

'There you are. I nearly sent out the search party,' she laughed.

'Who Churchill?' Caitlin chimed as the dog bounded towards her and jumped up to be made a fuss over. 'Hello boy, is your master away then?' she said.

'Yes, finally. He wasn't going to go, but I had encouraged him to do so,' Betty said as they headed down a dimly lit hallway towards the kitchen.

*Wasn't going to go*? *Hm* she thought, *why not?* If he planned to save his fortune, then he would not hesitate, but everything was heresy at the moment until she heard it from his mouth.

'I've brought the wine,' said Lynn, putting the carrier bag on the kitchen counter. 'I figured that if we were going to see ghosts then I'd rather do it drunk,' she laughed and went to the cupboard for glasses.

'Lynn, one look at you swaying down the corridors intoxicated would frighten them more than they could possibly frighten you,' Betty burst out laughing.

'So have you ever actually seen one, then?' Lynn asked Caitlin, who was fiddling with a little radio she brought in an attempt to communicate.

'Many times. I always saw them when I was a kid and it just intensified as I became older and started hanging around old houses and castles a lot as part of my job. I'm telling you there's something here, and it wants to talk...'

Lynn shivered. 'Oh now I'm worried.'

'*You* are worried?' cried Betty. 'I've got to live here,' she then laughed and looked nervously around the room as if something was about to pounce on her.

# Chapter Eleven

'Shall we put the lights out everywhere?' asked Betty.

'Why not?' Caitlin already had an inkling where most of the activity was taking place and it was in the bedroom at the front of the property. Why she knew this, she wasn't quite sure, but her instincts, thus far, haven't steered her wrong.

'But how we are going to capture evidence for Edward? I mean, it's not like we can suck them in a trap, is it? It isn't the movies. I mean, we don't have a trap for starters anyway, even if they exist, that is.' Lynn, already sipping wine, looked confused when Caitlin handed her a small, handheld camera.

'Use this...'

'It'll be shaky evidence if she drinks anymore tonight,' Laughed Betty as they headed to the bottom of the grand staircase.

'All we need is something moving, a sound or a capture of an actual entity. If he says then that we faked it, he's going to be the fourth Ghostbuster another night,' said Caitlin.

'Oh, Edward's afraid of the dark,' Betty said as the ascended the stairs. 'I don't think he'd be up for ghost hunting, I'm afraid.'

Caitilin was surprised to hear this. 'No way? Isn't he about my age?'

'Yes. Ever since he was a little boy. He couldn't stand this place and when he went to University, he vowed never to come back but then his father died...'

'That is interesting. Did you ever find out why he's afraid of the dark?' Lynn asked as they arrived on the landing that was eerily cold.

'No, he never ever wanted to talk about it. Some nights I've caught him sleeping with the lights on and television.'

Caitlin and Lynn laughed at this.

'But he's adamant he doesn't believe in ghosts,' Caitin said, finding the whole thing odd now knowing what she knows.

'So he says,' Betty said, opening the door of one of the bedrooms. 'This was his father's and his father's room...'

Betty put the lights on for a moment so they could get their bearings and you didn't need to sense ghosts to find the whole room rather creepy. The furniture was Victorian and dark, and the rugs looked faded and dusty. The four-poster bed had its curtains drawn, and they all looked at each other as if to say who'd be the first to open them.

'Let me,' said Caitlin, cautiously approaching the bed. With a swift hand, she pulled the curtain open to a made bed and nothing else. 'Sorted. Now, are we ok?' she asked, and they both nodded. 'How are you going to cope on Saturday during our walk?' she chuckled and switched on the radio.

'There's safety in numbers,' Lynn piped up and involuntarily shivered. 'Oh heck, it's gone cold in here, hasn't it?' Bet, have you left a window open?'

'No, I never come in here,' she responded, which Caitlin guessed by the dust in the room.

The radio began crackling, and they all fell silent and stared at it.

'Is there anyone here who would like to communicate?' asked Caitlin. 'Don't be afraid, we're...'

'Just a bunch of old women.' Added Lynn with a nervous laugh.

'Speak for yourself,' Caitlin chuckled.

'Yes, I'm not old, thank you,' Betty said. '63 is the new 40...'

Just then, a voice came through the radio, but it was indecipherable.

'Lynn, are you filming?' asked Caitlin.

'Yes,' she whispered.

'Hello, could you say it again please because it didn't come through clearly enough for us to understand?'

'Alfred,' it said.

At that moment, Betty gasped. 'That's my nephew in law's name...'

'Edward's father?' Caitlin said, feeling a bit shocked herself. 'Hello, Alfred, are you at peace? Do you have a message you'd like to share?' she asked, sensing something around her.

'There's three...of us,' it said.

'Three? Who are the others with you, Alfred? Can you tell us and why you're hanging around the castle? I'm sure it was you I saw the first day I came here.'

'To...right...wrongs,' it replied.

'Oh god,' cried Betty. 'I think I know what he means.'

Caitlin had an inkling too, but she needed more information than this, she needed specifics. 'What wrongs? You can use my phone's battery for energy if you need it. Please, Alfred, can you tell me what happened?'

'Amy...Daisy...Debra...'

'Who are they?' she asked Betty.

There was silence before Betty answered: 'They're his sisters,' she said. 'They were all estranged because of the debacle over the ownership of the castle. They believed it should've gone to...'

With that a loud bang of the front door followed, making them all jump. Lynn screamed and threw the light on. 'It's like that bloody Charles Dicken's story, Scrooge. Who's come to talk to us now! Past, future, or present!'

'I thought I locked the door,' cried Betty, and rushed out of the room. Standing on the landing overlooking the entrance hall they saw Edward's face, lit up by his mobile light, looking up at them with a baffled expression.

'It's the bloody present,' Caitlin muttered. 'Hi, Edward. I mean, you *are* really Edward, aren't you?' she asked, thinking he'd be halfway to London by now.

'Honestly, you three. What the bloody hell are you up to?' he asked. 'This place is as dark as a blackhole.' He shone his mobile torch onto the three of them.

They all looked at each other. 'Nothing,' replied Lynn, hiccoughing. 'Thought we'd do a bit of...stargazing.' She looked up at the ceiling.

'Inside the castle? God, Lynn, I thought you were more intelligent than that,' he shook his head and switched on the hallway lights. 'Come on, I want to talk to you all in the living room.'

'Oh god,' said Lynn. 'Do you think he's going to send us to the dungeon?' she laughed cheekily as they walked down the stairs.

'Do you have a dungeon?' Caitlin asked Betty, who was holding onto the rail as she walked down.

'Yes, we do, but nobody has been in there for donkey's ears.'

'Wow, I can imagine the dust,' Caitlin said, and they all laughed.

# Chapter Twelve

'I specifically asked you not to investigate,' he said, pacing the living room while the three of them were sitting on the sofa like scolded children.

'I'm sorry, it was my idea, and these two tagged along...'

'No, Caitlin,' said Betty. 'It was mine, I allowed them in here, Ed. I was curious too, and I thought if we found anything here, we could convince you to add the castle to the tour. We need the money to get this place fixed up.'

'I know we do,' he said calmly and sat down opposite them on the arm of the chair. 'I need a word with Caitlin, if possible, alone...would you both mind leaving us for a bit?' he asked, and they both agreed and left for the kitchen but not before Lynn threw a cheeky wink at Caitlin which Edward saw.

'I know we went against your wishes, but if you'd just listen to this, please...'

He held up his hand as if to shush her and went into his briefcase that was sitting on the coffee table and pulled out a file. 'You don't need to apologise for anything. The reason I didn't want you investigating the castle is because...'

'Because?'

'This is difficult for me to say so bear with me.' He got up and paced the room.

'Take all the time you need,' she said and sunk back into the comfortable sofa. She had an inkling where this was going after

46

many years of encountering and interviewing people who have experience the paranormal but struggled to accept what they had saw. After a couple of minutes he sat back down on the chair.

'I know there is something here because it scared the living daylights out of me when I was a youngster. It still does if I'm honest. When I was twelve, I had an experience I've never managed to forget...'

*Now this was making sense*, she thought.

'Oh, really... Can I ask what?' At this point she sat up eagerly waiting for more.

He took out a sheet of paper from the file. 'I was alone one night in my room that was next to my father's when I saw a lady standing by the fireplace who looked as real as you and me. I thought nothing of it, she seemed friendly and maybe I didn't hear her come in...or so I thought. She told me one thing and then disappeared before my very eyes...'

'What did she say?'

'She said the castle belonged to Holly very angrily and then left.'

Caitlin covered her mouth in shock. 'Oh my god...'

'Since then I have hated sleeping here, but I was curious about her allegation,' he laughed at this point. 'I had forgotten about it until my father died and I began questioning things...so over the last few months while I was trying to sell this place, I had a guilty conscience and asked a lawyer friend to look into it. Caitlin, this castle should've been Holly's as the first child of Alfred's...' He handed her the document.

'Wow,' she whispered.

'You don't seem as surprised as I thought you'd be?'

Of course she wasn't as she'd already found it out before she came and was hoping to speak with Betty on the quiet but now that it was all out in the open...

'I did my own research. In fact, I only found Holly's writings tonight up in the attic. The reason she spent so much time at the castle was because she knew the truth.'

'I had a feeling she did somehow, but she never ever said a word to my dad about it, which I thought was strange.'

'Perhaps she thought too fondly of you all to cause a fuss?'

'That would explain it actually, as she was that sort of woman. Now,' he sighed as if a great relief had been lifted off his shoulders. 'How do you feel being the owner of a castle?'

Everything she ever wanted was now hers, and she didn't know how to process it. 'I can't wrap my head around it really, but...this is your home. Your family home? I don't know how I feel about taking it...'

Edward laughed, got up from his seat, and sat down next to her. 'It's rightfully yours. When I met you, I knew who you were as soon as you said you were Holly's last living relative, so I had my man check it out and it's yours. So best to start planning those ghost tours,' he chuckled and nudged her friendly on the arm.

'But what about Betty? This is her home. I mean, she can stay of course... I... I don't really know what to think at the moment or what to do, but...thank you for being honest.' It was then she realised why there was sadness in his eyes the previous day.

He lowered his head, hands clasped together on his legs. 'I had to right the wrongs of my family. I could never have lived with myself if I had sold this and not spoken up. Now, it's too bad that I can't ask you out on a date because it also turns out that we're related in some way.'

She put her hand on his. 'But we can be friends, can't we?'

'Caitlin, we can be the best of friends. Come on, let's go tell the news to Betty as no doubt this will run through the village like a wildfire before sunrise...'

# Chapter Thirteen

Putting her key into the lock of the cottage door, she couldn't quite believe what had just happened. 'Winston,' she called and put the light on to find him walking casually down the stairs. 'Oh there you are, come here,' she said, scooping him up into her arms. 'You'll never guess what's happened, Win. We're the proud owners of the castle. A castle! Can you believe it? No, neither can I.' She was about to head into the kitchen to feed him when there was a knock at the door. 'One moment,' she said, looking at the clock on the wall. 'Who is calling at 2.30 am?' she wondered and when she opened the door there was a loud squealing noise from Patricia and Harry dressed in their nightclothes.

'We just heard, and we couldn't contain our excitement for you, so we had to drop by and say this is amazing news for the village. How do you feel?'

'Thanks guys. I'm still wrapping my head around it all. Do you want to come in?' she asked.

'Oh gosh no, love. It's late. Just pop by the Sceptre tomorrow at lunchtime, all right?' Patricia said.

'Of course, I'll see you then,' she said, and they said their goodnights and left.

Closing the door and locking it, she then fed Winston and headed to bed, but lying in the dark with the moonlight shining through the window and the view of the castle, she couldn't quite believe her luck.

'Thank you, Holly,' she whispered and snuggled under the duvet.

She awoke the following morning to many messages on her phone from residents who had her number from her advert and many emails enquiring about her walk, having heard on the grapevine about her new inheritance. 'They weren't joking when they said word gets around fast here,' she said and sat up. For the next few hours she began writing up the castle into her tour and thought she'd better take a look around to see what else she could offer as her number one priority right now was to help the local businesses and her new-found friends. As she was about to get up, a message came through from Edward asking her if she wanted to take Winston for a walk.

**Yes, that'll be brilliant. I'll see you in about an hour at the bottom of my drive.**

**I'll bring us a coffee flask and breakfast. We can have it by the lake.**

She smiled at this, having found family, at last, but there was a sadness too knowing she and Edward couldn't be anything more than just that no matter how distant they were in the family tree. She got showered and dressed and headed downstairs, replying to yet more messages and enquiries mainly for the Halloween tour she hadn't yet planned out, but now there was a castle involved she knew she had to go one step further. 'Come on, Win. Let's get you fed,' she said, noticing Edward walking up the drive with Churchill already.

'Morning,' she opened the door to them before he could knock.

'Been hiding from the paparazzi, have you?' he laughed.

'More like excited villagers,' she smiled, but it didn't bother her in the slightest. 'Do you want to come in...'

'I'm ready if you're ready.'

'Sure, let me just get Winston,' she said and as soon as he saw Edward, he got his harness on without a fuss. 'Wow I think you're a good influence on him.'

'I have that effect on animals,' he smiled. As they walked down the drive, he asked, 'How does it feel to own a castle?'

'Weird. I still can't believe it. But what about you? What will you do now?'

'Probably head back to London and do what I've always done. Be a lawyer,' he said with a touch of sadness in his voice.

'Won't you miss it here?' she asked, picking Winston up when she saw a tractor approaching.

'Of course, but in the meantime, if there's anything I can help you with, just ask. Oh, and you have free legal advice and representation, anyway. I'll help sort out the transfer of ownership and whatnot.'

'Oh you don't have to...'

'We're friends, okay and that's what we do.'

'Family.'

Disappointment washed over his face at those words. 'Yes, family,' he said with a tinge of bitterness that she couldn't hardly miss.

'Good morning,' hollered John from the tractor. 'And what do I hear this morning? That we have a new owner of the castle? Oh sorry Ed...' he added.

'Nah, that's quite all right. I'm happy for her.'

'Thanks, John. It's surreal if I'm honest.'

'I bet it is. Well, I hope to see you both at the Sceptre lunchtime. I don't know what's going on, but I had a message at 6 am to be there,' he laughed. 'Good job I'm up at the crack of dawn anyway.'

'We'll be there,' said Edward.

'Well, later then,' he waved and turned into his field.

'What is exactly going on at the pub?' she asked.

'I'm not quite sure, to be honest. Betty told me this morning to be there that's all.'

Sitting on a wooden bench overlooking the lake and surrounded by trees, Edward went into his rucksack and pulled out a plastic lunchbox. 'Betty made it this morning. It's pumpkin cake with the pumpkins from John's farm. Do you want a slice?' he asked. 'I have to admit I ate two slices for breakfast,' he laughed and patted his flat stomach. 'I think I'd better hit the gym when I get back to London.'

'Love some,' she said, thinking of another idea to go along with the walk. 'When are you going back?'

'When all the paperwork is wrapped up, I suppose.'

'How does Betty feel?' she asked, thinking she'd let her still live there and work. She thought perhaps she could open a café in one of the living rooms.

'She's ecstatic for you, couldn't be happier. I think she's afraid of losing her home though, if I'm honest.'

'I don't want her to go anywhere, you can tell her that.'

'I'm so happy to hear that. You can tell her in a couple of hours at the pub. So, when is this ghost walk of yours then?'

'Saturday. Are you thinking of joining us?' she playfully nudged his arm. 'Oh come on, you may learn a thing or two.'

He laughed. 'Of course I'm coming. I want to see what all the fuss has been about and learn a thing or two, of course.'

'Shame you're related,' said Harry to her once she arrived outside the pub.

'Huh?' she said, confused at what he was talking about.

'You and Edward.'

'Oh, well, I suppose it is, but that's life, I guess,' she shrugged. 'So what's happening?' she asked, indicating to the pub.

He smiled. 'Come on, you'll see.'

# Chapter Fourteen

'Surprise!' the villagers shouted in unison as she walked through the door.

*Is it my birthday?* she thought and looked up above the bar. There was a banner strung across the shelf filled with empty glasses which said: 'Congratulations! And Thank You For Saving The Village!'

She touched her chest at the heartfelt gesture and was about to cry when Lynn and Patricia bounded forward from the crowd and hugged her in turn.

'You didn't have to do this!' she cried, as Harry brought her over a glass of wine.

'Yes, we did,' said Harry.

'It's not much,' said Lynn,' But we feel this ghost walk tour and your new status as the castle owner will do wonders for the village and businesses.' At this moment, she noticed Edward standing next to Caitlin grinning. 'Oh, no offence, Ed...'

'No,' he chuckled. 'None taken, ladies. I think the place is in good hands.' He pulled out a chair for Caitlin and then sat down himself.

'Wow. I've never had a surprise party like this. I don't know what to say,' she said and took a sip of the wine. 'Gosh it's a bit too early for this, isn't it?'

'Not here, love,' John laughed.

'It's wine o'clock anytime of the day here,' Lynn laughed and sat down next to them at the table. 'So what plans have you got for the castle?' she asked excitedly as the whole pub listened.

Caitlin looked at Edward, who smiled at her. His dark eyes oozing with pride. 'Oh, lots. Maybe a café for Betty...' she said and at this Betty shrieked.

'Oh my god, if we could pull it off that would be an absolute dream,' she said.

'First of all we need to make some money. Serious money. How many rooms are closed to the public?' she asked Edward.

'At least two of the rooms downstairs and the ballroom, but other than that, it's safe. I have the surveyor's papers.'

'Right,' she nodded, thinking.

'Got some ideas?' he asked.

'Yep. Leave it with me.' She picked up her glass and took another sip of the wine. 'Actually, does anyone know how to set up a website? I think we should add a Night At The Castle theme to the tour and offer bed and breakfast with a ghost tour until 3 am or something,' she said as the ideas whizzed around her head.

'My son loves all that stuff,' said John. 'I'll ask him. Want me to send him over later to sort it out for you?'

'Yes, that would be fantastic, thank you.'

'And I'll start sorting the rooms we have available,' said Betty. 'Most just need a dust.'

'What else have you got planned, Caitlin?' asked Edward as they strolled back to her cottage along the country road. 'I know you won't just stop at that,' he smiled.

'Oh, that would be telling, wouldn't it?' They halted as the castle came into view and both looked fondly over at it.

'Are you sad to let it go?' she asked. 'I mean, really sad?'

'Nope. I'm glad. I never wanted it and that's the truth. Having to tell friends I lived in a castle while they had a normal, modern two up and down was an embarrassment. No, I like things less grandeur, I'm afraid. I'm not like my father at all,' he chuckled.

'I love it for its history. When you walk around the halls in the presence of many great people and battles that must've taken place here, it's amazing...'

She caught Edward sneaking a glance at her. 'I know you're the right person for it and I think Holly, if she's watching now, knew that too, somehow...'

'Thanks. Coming in for pumpkin cake?' she asked.

'Sure, why not? It's quite addicting,' he shrugged, and they walked up the drive to see a man in a suit about to walk down the drive.

'Oh, hello. Can I help you?' she asked.

'Yes, I was told a Mr. Edward Thomas would be here.'

'I'm Edward. How can I help?' he said.

'I have some news for you from your lawyer. He has asked me to deliver this personally. Sorry, I haven't introduced myself. I'm Geoffry Tate, a local genealogist.'

'A genealogist? Okay, that's interesting,' he said with a baffled expression. 'He didn't tell me he had spoken to you.'

'You're welcome to come inside, if you want?' Caitlin asked, about to unlock the front door with her key.

'Er, sure, come on inside,' said Edward looking confused. He exchanged a glance with Caitlin as the man went into the house. Caitlin shrugged, not having a clue what was going on either.

'Can I take your coat?' she asked.

'That would be great, thank you,' he said, shrugging off his jacket and handing it to her.

'Cup of tea? Pumpkin cake?' she offered.

'Oh that would be lovely, thank you.'

'So,' Edward sat down on the opposite chair. 'Why did Brian send you?' he asked.

'I have some very important news for you.' He opened his briefcase. 'He reached out to me when you enquired about the ownership of the castle...'

Edward leaned forward in his chair. 'He did? He didn't mention anything to me.'

'No. He asked me to look into it very carefully before he said anything.' He pulled two sheets of paper from his case and closed it. 'I think you will find this most interesting, Mr Thomas.' Caitlin handed him a small plate with a slice of cake on it and put his cup of tea on the coffee table. While Geoffry broke a slice off with a fork, Caitlin sat on the arm of the chair wondering what was going on.

'What would that be?' Edward asked.

'Well, it seems that your father shouldn't had taken over ownership of the castle after his father had died because, well, I am sorry to have to tell you this...he wasn't the rightful heir. Your father was adopted from a local family. I'm sorry, Mr Thomas.' He handed him the paper. 'Your father was the son of Miriam and Donald Jones.'

'Oh my god,' Caitlin whispered and covered her mouth with her hands. This was very last thing she expected to hear today.

'Splendid cake, by the way,' Geoffry said and cleared his plate. 'Very seasonal...'

# Chapter Fifteen

After Geoffry had left with the rest of the cake wrapped in foil, Caitlin closed the door and turned to Edward, sitting on the chair stock still in disbelief. Did she hear right? Was she and Edward no longer related?

'Um, Edward,' she said, returning to the living room. 'Can I get you anything? A drink? More cake?' she asked, wondering how cake would help right now, but who could say no cake. Maybe he'd need a dash of whiskey in his coffee too with news like this.

He rose from his seat slowly and walked to the fireplace. 'No, thank you, Caitlin. I um... I don't know what to think right now.' He looked up into the mirror and saw her reflection staring back at him. They locked eyes for a moment, and then he turned to face her. 'We're not...I mean, we're not family in that sense of the word...'

Caitlin felt a crack of her heart at the words. She had so longed to find family, and now it was taken away from her again. She shook her head, tears streaming down her cheeks. 'No, I guess we're not.' She sat down on the sofa thinking she was just meant to be alone in the world when Edward walked slowly towards her before getting down on his knees in front of her. 'Caitlin,' he whispered, taking her hand in his. 'Do you know what this means?'

She raised her head and looked into his tear-filled eyes. 'What?' she asked.

'It means I can be honest with you now. From the moment I saw you on the road that morning, I liked you, more than liked to be honest, but I had to stuff my feelings down when I discovered what I did. No matter how distant cousins we may have been. Yet, there was something in my heart that told me it couldn't had been right because what I felt and have been feeling was too strong. So what if I'm related to the Jones's,' he laughed. 'If it means we can be more than friends, I'm the happiest person alive.' He brushed a strand of her hair away from her face.

She cried at this and rested her head on his shoulder. 'I would love that,' she smiled into his shoulder and inhaled his woody scent. 'I'm really glad too, if I'm honest.' She lifted her head and placed her hands on his stubby face. 'I may not have family now, but I gained something better,' she leaned forward and placed a kiss on his lips, which he returned with more vigour.

She awoke on the Saturday with a spring in her step. Today was the day she had been preparing for, her guided walking tours of Grantham Village. When she checked her phone, she saw that it was fully booked way past Halloween, including the packaged deal, but she knew she had to prepare something spectacular for that day and help bring more business in for the locals.

'Want a coffee?' shouted Edward from the kitchen. Caitlin picked up her file from her desk that she had finally put together the previous night. 'Yes, thanks,' she replied as she walked down the stairs. Edward came out of the kitchen with two mugs and a grumpy looking Winston following behind him. He placed a kiss on her forehead and handed her the mug. 'How are you feeling this morning?' he asked and sat down on the sofa, warming his feet by the electric fire.

'Excited. Plus I've worked out what I'm doing for Halloween at the castle. I wondered if you could help me sort a few things out.'

'Of course, anything now I'm not going back to London.'

'You're not?' she said, surprised but equally happy to hear it.

'No. I'll find something to do here. But not being a lawyer,' he laughed. 'Have you got any jobs at the castle?' he asked, winking.

'Now you've come to mention it...' she smiled and handed him a piece of paper.

'What's this plan of yours then?' he asked and looked at what she'd written. 'Wow. Okay, this sounds bloody brilliant. I will get on to it ASAP and rope in Harry and John.'

She bent down to kiss him. 'Thank you.'

It was late afternoon when she ventured into the village and was shocked to find it busy with people mulling around waiting for the tour to start. She went into the shop to find Lynn flat out serving customers and beckoned her over to have a word. Lynn called Patricia over who was filling the shelves with pumpkin jam, who then took over the reins at the till.

'Hi, love,' said Lynn, exasperated. 'It's been nonstop busy here since 10 a.m. What have you done to our little village?' she asked with a smile.

'I've woken it up,' she laughed. 'I've got a few things up my sleeve for Halloween and wondered if you could ask other business owners if they'd be interested in selling their wares at the Halloween Castle Fayre. Let's blow this whole thing up. Let's go wild...'

'Yes, absolutely I will sort it out. I heard all the rooms at the castle have been sold for Halloween at £500 a ticket! It's gone crazy!'

Caitlin nodded, hardly believing it herself. 'I know. I don't know how on earth it has gone so well...'

'I may be able to help with that,' shouted Patricia from the till. 'Harry made a video on TikTok and YouTube about it. Didn't he tell you?'

'No!' said Caitlin hardly surprised to hear it was Harry. 'I'll have a look.' She went onto her phone and there was Harry's cheeky self, standing outside the castle with a Ghostbuster T-shirt on. 'Oh my god,' she laughed. 'Good on you, Harry...'

'Oh and I believe you have something else to tell us as well?' Lynn said with a wink.

'What?' she asked, thinking she'd forgotten something important.

'You and Edward, that's what! It's the talk of the bloody village.'

'Betty told us,' said Patricia. 'How long do you think she'd keep that quiet, eh?'

'News does spread like wildfire here, doesn't it?' she laughed.

# Chapter Sixteen

Caitlin checked her phone. It was now almost 5 pm and so she, Betty and Edward headed to the meeting point outside Lynn's shop where everyone was to meet to start the tour. She had done walking tours many times before in the past, but none had been as special as this, so her nerves were starting to show.

'You're going to be fine,' said Edward, taking her hand in his. 'I'm so proud of you,' he gave her hand a squeeze.

'Thank you,' she whispered as they came to a halt on the pavement.

'Go break a leg,' he said giving her a gentle push forward.

She cleared her throat. 'Good evening, everyone,' she said with a slightly raised voice so they could hear at the back of a very large crowd of people, including teenagers and kids. 'Thanks for being here. We're going to start our walk at this shop and it's for a very special reason...not because Lynn sells the best cakes, but because over 400 years ago this building was once owned by a witch...'

There were gasps from the crowd, and even Lynn's mouth fell open with shock. 'Really?' she said.

'Yep, follow me,' she said and headed across the road to the farm. 'Juiper was her name, and she was the deemed to be the first resident of Grantham Village. In fact, she made the village what it is today...'

There were murmurs of surprise from the crowd.

'It's a little-known fact, but it's true. Then, unfortunately,' she turned to face the crowd, 'the witch trials began, and Juniper was hung on this field. Tell me, if you're a long-term resident here, have you encountered anything strange on Halloween around these parts?' she asked. She looked around the crowd, at the residents. John was looking at his son, who was urging him to speak.

'I have, yes,' he raised his hand. At this point, everyone turned to face him.

'Tell us, John, we'd love to hear it,' she said, wondering what it could be. She'd only dug this information out after a friend from university had sent her some old manuscripts written by a local monk.

'Well,' he cleared his throat. 'I can tell you a story about last Halloween. I was locking up the gates after I had gotten a call to say they were open, and several horses were going walkabout when I heard a woman crying. So I look around and there's nobody there. Thinking I'm losing the plot, I head home on foot down there,' he pointed to the road past the castle. 'Not long after I hear footsteps behind me, and I turn around and see a young woman with a hood over head clasping her hands together as if begging for help. I said, 'are you alright?' and then she disappeared before my very eyes. Naturally, I ran all the way to the front door. Scared me so much I hate coming out here at night,' he laughed nervously. 'But oddly enough, my pumpkins this year have been the best they've ever been...'

'Wow, so you've seen a full-on apparition, then? Consider yourself lucky and maybe the pumpkins were a gift for acknowledging her.'

'I wouldn't say I was lucky at the time,' he said, and the crowd laughed.

'Let's move on to the castle...'

When they arrived at the castle, Betty and Patricia invited everyone to a refreshment and a snack from the table laid out in the hallway.

'Come here,' said Edward, taking her hand and leading her into the library. 'While they're entertained a minute by Betty and Pat, I want to show you something.'

What is it?' she asked as they entered the huge room with shelves as far as the ceiling.

'My father collected books in his time, mainly fiction. I wondered if you would look through them one day and see if there's anything worth selling to help the castle...'

'Oh, Ed, they're your dad's. I don't want them to go...' she said, scanning the titles.

'They need looking after and it's fine. I know he would want to save the castle more than he would want me to keep the books...'

'You're not a reader?' she asked, pulling out something that caught her eye.

'Well...not much, I have to admit.'

She smiled. 'It's fine. We all have our areas of interest...Jesus a first copy of Dracula,' she gasped and when she turned the delicate page over there was a signature. 'Oh my god...this is signed by Stoker.'

'Worth anything?'

'I say!' she gasped, staring at the book in her hands.

'If I remember rightly, he did go for signatures so there may be more here, who knows.'

'God, Ed, you've had people walk in and out of here with all his lying around. I can't believe it. There could be thousands upon thousands of pounds' worth here,' she whispered. She carefully put the book back in the space on the shelf. 'Lock the doors, okay, not that I believe anyone would take anything but to be on the safe side. I know someone who is interested in antique books and will be interested in seeing this lot. Right,' she breathed out. 'Let's get back to the tour, shall we?'

'One more thing,' he said, pulling her towards him.

'What?' She looked up at him, smiling down at her.

He leaned closer to her and pressed a kiss on her lips.

'Ahem,' came a voice by the door, They both turned around. 'Your people are waiting,' said Lynn with a snigger.

# Chapter Seventeen

'And so we enter the second floor where King Richard the third stayed...' she said as she stood on top of the landing, waiting for everyone to gather around.

'He did?' asked Edward, who was standing to the side of her.

'Yes, don't you know anything?' she asked with a laugh.

'Seems like I need a personal history lesson,' he whispered in her ear. She smiled at this and regained her composure.

'It is ok if we go inside your father's room, is it?' she asked him.

'Of course, royalty stayed here,' he said with surprise. 'I think I want to see it for myself again now.'

With that, she beckoned the audience to follow her down the dark hallway and entered the bedroom that belonged to Edward's father. 'It's believed he stayed in here for a week but there is no information as to why he came here,' she said, shining her torch on the doorknob and then opening it. As she walked further into the room, the colder it got. Just then there was a clatter of something falling on the floor and everyone ran out of the room screaming except for Edward and Caitlin.

'What was that?' he asked, switching on the torch. He shone it on the dresser and then onto the floor.

'What's that?' she asked, seeing something small and red lying on the rug.

''Nothing,' he picked it up swiftly and put it in his pocket. 'Maybe the resident ghost threw it,' he laughed nervously at the thought that it could be his father.

'Seems like something hit it off whatever it was,' she said, calling the others back into the room. 'It looks like the activity has started. Lynn, could you pass me the cat balls, please. Let's see if we can get any intelligent responses.' She placed them on the bed and asked if anyone had a question they would to ask.

'Are you the King?' A young boy shouted and at that moment the lights flashed red for yes, and the whole audience gasped.

'That was a fun night,' said Edward, sat opposite her in Betty's kitchen. 'I had no idea about half of what you talked about. You sure know your history.' He picked up his mug of coffee.

'I studied it for long enough,' she smiled and then yawned.

'Here you go,' said Betty putting a stack of toast on the table. 'It's been so nice to see the castle full of life again. When's the next one?' she asked, wiping her hands on the tea towel thrown over her shoulder.

'Halloween now but there's a lot to organise between now and then...'

'That reminds me,' Ed put his mug down. 'I've started you know what, and I think it's going to be amazing.'

'Oh what are you talking about?' asked Betty, intrigued and leaning on the table.

'Shall I tell her?' Edward asked. Caitlin nodded. 'We're organising a Halloween ball. I just need to get one part of the roof fixed to make it safe and we're good to go...'

'A ball. Oh my god, how exciting. There hasn't been an event in this castle since your parents' wedding.'

'There hasn't?' he asked, surprised to hear it.

'No. When your mother passed on, your poor dad gave up too. As much as he loved this castle, his heart wasn't in it much anymore either. No wonder it started to fall into more disrepair.'

'That's a shame,' said Caitlin, pouring more coffee. 'But one thing at a time. The takings from last night will cover the roof repair so I'll now need to call in some favours for the décor and food but of course the tickets will cover it.'

'And call your book friend,' he reminded her.

'Oh what's this about?' Betty asked.

'He wants to sell his dad's books to raise funds for the castle. I told him no but...'

'I think it's a good idea. They're murder to keep dust free.'

'See, told you so,' Edward smiled.

'Right, okay, I'll call him this afternoon.'

# Chapter Eighteen

'If you could just sign here,' Edward asked, pointing at an empty line under his signature, 'and then the castle is yours.'

Holding her favourite pen in her hands, she took a deep breath before she committed her signature in ink. 'It's that easy,' she laughed nervously as the reality of owning such an amazing piece of history dawned on her.

'That easy,' he replied, watching her sign. 'How does it feel now?' he asked sitting down next to her on the sofa.

She picked up the piece of paper and then looked around the room, at the carved pumpkins on the fireplace with the candles flickering from the menacing eyes. 'Indescribable,' she whispered when she felt his hand on her knee.

'I guess I'll be paying rent today, eh?' he laughed.

At this point, she wondered what he was going to do as they hadn't discussed living arrangements yet.

'Well, I'm not evicting you, if that's what you mean? I think I would still like to live in Holly Cottage for the time being, but…you're welcome to join me, if you want?' she asked, afraid of what his reaction would be.

For a few intense moments, he looked lovingly into her eyes. 'I would really love that. What about Churchill? Will Winston agree?' he laughed and then reached over to plant a kiss on her nose.

'Winston needs to learn how to share,' she smiled. 'So, shall we get the Halloween ball sorted?' she leapt from the chair full of excitement and raring to go.

'Yes, let's get on with it. There's just two days to go. How time flies when you're having fun.' He draped his arm around her shoulders as they headed out into the hall.

'Hi, Harry,' she said as he was busy mopping the tiled floor.

'Is it done?' he asked, looking up.

'She waved the paper around. 'Yep. I'm your new boss!'

'Bloody fantastic. Oh, no offence, Ed,' he laughed cheekily.

'None taken, Harry. None at all.' He patted him on the shoulder. 'I'm glad you were able to keep your job, that's all.'

'Me too. The castle feels like home from home.' He went back to mopping the floor, whistling the Addams Family tune.

Later that afternoon, they strolled hand in hand down the lane to Holly Cottage. The sun was low in the sky and Farmer John was busy in his field with customers buying his pumpkins.

'I'm glad it worked out for him,' she said. 'Oh, is it true you are related?'

Edward laughed. 'Yes, we're cousins, who would've thought it. I used to drive past the field almost on a daily basis and we'd wave or say hello but never ever thought for one minute we'd be family. Funny how life turns out sometimes, isn't it?'

'Yeah, like going from living in a cottage to a castle in less than a month,' she laughed and leaned into him.

'Or going from living alone in a humongous house, except for Betty of course to finding love and downsizing to a cute cottage with Winston Churchill,' he laughed. 'I mean with Winston and Churchill but,' he halted on the path and turned to her. 'But most of all you...'

'You're just being nice,' she said.

'No, trust me, I'm not,' he said and kissed her hard on the lips. 'I'm a lawyer, we don't play nice...'

'Ex lawyer,' she reminded him, and they continued walking to the cottage she could now see peeking from the trees on the hill. 'So have you decided what you'll do now?' she asked.

'I said I'd help John on the farm for a bit. I've had enough of stuffy offices and courtrooms; I think it's time for some outdoors.'

'But tonight, let's have a night in, shall we? I need time to sit and think.'

'What? Time to sit and think you own a castle or have the nicest boyfriend in the world?' he joked with a playful nudge on her arm.

'Both,' she replied.

# Chapter Nineteen

The Sceptre was busy the following evening with the residents milling around and chatting about the Halloween ball and fayre at the castle the following day. Edward brought a drink over from the busy bar and put it on the table before sitting down opposite her.

'I've never seen this place so alive,' he said. 'Shall we just have this last one and get back to the castle? I think we've got a few more decorations to hang.'

'Oh that reminds me,' she said, putting down her glass. 'The foam gravestones. I need to stick them in the front lawn...'

'Don't worry, Harry and John saw to that this afternoon. Lynn and Betty have been busy making pumpkin cakes all day and Patricia and a few local girls have been cleaning the rooms ready...' He placed a hand on hers. 'Don't worry. It's looking good.'

'This *is* going to work, isn't it?' she asked, but she had a knowing it would.

'It's going to be even better than you imagined.' He finished his drink, put the glass on the table and pulled on his coat. 'Come on, we've still got work to do. By the way...' he asked as they walked out of the pub into the cool breeze. 'What are you dressing up as?'

'Now that would be telling, wouldn't it?'

When she entered the castle, she gasped. 'Oh wow...' The edges of the hall were lined with pumpkins and fake, silvery glittery cobwebs were dangling from the ceiling hitting the lights from the chandeliers. The red carpet on the staircase was clean and fresh, with candles running along the sides. 'It's like something from Harry Potter,' she said, walking around staring at all the decorations.

'It is rather. Although, if I'm honest I've never seen a film...'

'Never?' She was shocked. 'Okay, well that's our evening sorted then,' she smiled and headed to the kitchen to see Betty. Before she even got within an inch of the kitchen, the sound of laughter and the smell of cake permeated the air of the ancient hall. 'Hello?' she intoned as pushed open the kitchen door to find the women sitting around decorating cupcakes for the kids.

'Hey,' said Lynn excitedly. 'We wondered when you'd join us. Pull up a pew and get icing,' she said.

At that moment, Edward came in with a serious look on his face. 'Um, we have a visitor,' he said, directing it to Caitlin.

'Oh?' she looked up from the table and put her icing bag down. 'Who?'

'Oh no, not the bloody ghosts again,' cried Betty, and they all laughed.

'No, a real human. Come on,' he said. 'I think you may want to meet her.'

She got off the chair, wondering what on earth was going on. They weren't expecting the paying guests until the morning. Heading out of the kitchen Patricia, Betty and Lynn followed behind.

'Who could it be?' Lynn whispered.

'No idea,' Caitlin shrugged. She followed Edward into the living room and halted by the door when she saw the back of an older woman sitting on the sofa.

'Ed, what's going on?' she asked as the woman rose from her seat and turned around.

Edward came towards her, smiling. 'Caitlin, I would like you to meet Rosie. Rosie is your mother's second cousin.'

There were shocks and gasps from behind her. 'My mother's...how?' She stared at the woman with piercing blue eyes and grey hair cut into a bob.

'I asked Tate to look into for you before he left that day. As it turns out, you do have some family left,' he said.

Rosie stepped towards her with her hand outstretched. 'It's so lovely to meet you, Caitlin. I'm sorry our families never stayed in touch or anything...'

'Oh my god,' she whispered. 'It's so lovely to meet you and you really do look like my mother,' she began to cry.

Rosie pulled her in for a hug. 'If I had known Lily had a family, I would've looked for them, but our families didn't really get on that well and so everyone lost touch over the years. Lily and I were like best friends growing up and I always wondered what became of her...'

'Another picture for your wall,' said Patricia lovingly.

# Chapter Twenty

'Happy Halloween, my ghost queen,' shouted Edward from downstairs.

'Do you know that sounded so cheesy even Winston is looking mortified,' she laughed as she put the finishing touches to her make-up.

'Winston always looks mortified, hon,' he replied.

That's true, she thought, rubbing his head as he sat on her dressing table. After she swiped the red lipstick on her lips, she stood up to appraise her appearance. Dressed in a black dress with freshly dyed black hair and pale make-up she thought she made the perfect vampire to welcome guests to her haunted castle for the evening. She picked up Winston and went downstairs to find Edward dressed as... 'Edward from Twilight?' she laughed hard at this and thought she needed to take pictures right now for the girls to see.

'Well it's my namesake, isn't it?' he laughed. 'Besides, the last time I dressed up for Halloween was when I was six, so I don't have much experience in these matters.'

'Looks like it. I'm not sure you're going to scare many people like that but come on, we need to go and get the place ready. Guests will be arriving at midday.' She picked up her bag and folder off the arm of the chair and they walked down the path towards the castle. The area was already busy with cars and people walking around in ghoulish costumes. 'If only every day was like this,' she mused and thought to herself that since she owned the castle it could.

'No thanks,' replied Edward, indicating to his outfit. 'Oh, I forgot the glitter,' he slapped his forehead.

'Glitter?' she asked.

'Don't the vampires sparkle in the daylight?'

She rolled her eyes and carried on walking. Outside the castle the tables were set up with produce from the local artisans and businesses and people were already slowly coming in for a browse.

'It's going swimmingly,' said Harry dressed as Lurch from the Addams Family. 'And a few guests have arrived now and are waiting to check in.'

'Thanks, Harry. Great costume. Maybe you could be on the doors' this evening then.'

'Youuu rannngg?' he said, and they fell about in fits of laughter.

'This is amazing,' Edward said as he went inside. While Edward went to tend something in the kitchen, Caitlin went to the reception where Betty was flipping through the diary.

'This is incredible, isn't it?' she said.

'Wait until you see this,' she said, handing her the book. 'We're booked for next Halloween too and every month in between. The phone has been ringing all day. I think we need to hire a receptionist,' she said seriously.

'Really?' she flipped through the book. 'Oh my god, looks like I'll be doing host tours pretty much every night. Betty, I think I'd better train people to do this as I'd never have a day off in...' she went through the book. 'Fifteen months.'

'What about John's boys? They're good lads and the two of them are old enough?'

'Sounds like a plan, I think.'

'THRILLERRRRR    THRILLLERRR    NIGHTTSS...' Rang out from the speakers as the hall filled with people dressed in everything from ghosts to banshees to zombies. Edward took her hand and dragged her onto the dancefloor. 'Come on, I love this song,' he said as everyone got into step and did the Thriller dance.

'I thought you'd be too stuffy for this sort of music,' she smiled.

'What? You clearly have a lot to learn about me, miss.'

'Good job you're living at the cottage then.'

'Yes, good job, isn't it? Stay there...' he said and left her standing alone on the dancefloor. Several moments later, the music stopped, and everyone came to a standstill wondering what was going on. At that moment, *A Love Song For A Vampire* came on and Edward walked across the dancefloor towards her, the crowd dispersing as he did so until there were only two of them standing under a glitter ball. He took her hands and then got down on one knee.

Surprised and not expecting this at0 all, she found herself closing her eyes thinking it all had to be a dream.

Edward reached into his trouser pocket and produce a red little box which she remembered from the ghost tour.

'Is that...?'

'Yes, it fell on the floor in my father's room. Now, I'm not a believer in this stuff like you, but I believe that night he was trying to tell me something...' With that he opened the box revealing a glittering emerald ring. 'This was my mother's and before that it was my father's mothers. I know it's been a very short time, but I don't think time counts when you're in love. Cailtin, I'm asking if you would be my wife...'

The audience began clapping and whooping.

'Oh my god,' she whispered, staring at the ring. Winston toddled towards her and rubbed her legs before going up to the ring, sniffing it as if giving his approval and miaowed at Edward.

'I think he agrees,' he said and took the ring out of the box and taking her hand.

'So, will you be my wife?'

'Yes, I will be wife,' she cried.

**IF YOU ENJOYED THIS BOOK YOU MAY ALSO LIKE:**

Christmas Spells and Jingle Bells

The Christmas Guest

Milton Keynes UK
Ingram Content Group UK Ltd.
UKHW041819211123
432980UK00001BB/58